The Extra Nose

WRITTEN BY
DANIEL DiPRIMA

ILLUSTRATED BY
BETH AND TODD PERSCHE

Zino Press
CHILDREN'S BOOKS
Middleton, Wisconsin

CHILDREN'S BOOKS

A Division of Knowledge Unlimited, Inc.

2348 Pinehurst Drive
Middleton, WI 53562
800 356-2303

THE EXTRA NOSE
Text © 1994 by Daniel DiPrima
Illustrations © 1994 by Zino Press Children's Books
Illustrations and design by Beth and Todd Persche
Printed in the U.S.A.

ISBN 1-55933-149-6

Library of Congress Catalog Card Number 94-60471

For Zaydie.

ONE DAY WHILE CROSSING THE STREET
I CAME ACROSS A TREAT.
AN EXTRA NOSE
LAY AT MY TOES!
I NEARLY FROZE.

SUCH A FIND CANNOT BE TAKEN LIGHTLY.
AFTER ALL, ONE DOESN'T FIND SPARE NOSES NIGHTLY!

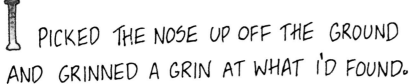

I PICKED THE NOSE UP OFF THE GROUND
AND GRINNED A GRIN AT WHAT I'D FOUND.

"NOW I HAVE AN EXTRA NOSE, IN CASE
I LOSE THE ONE THAT'S ON MY FACE.
I'LL NEVER HAVE TO WORRY
IF I NEED ANOTHER IN A HURRY."

I HELD THE NOSE AND THOUGHT A WHILE
AND SOON MY GRIN BECAME A SMILE.

OR I COULD USE THEM BOTH AT ONCE
AND SMELL THE SMELLS WITH TWICE THE SCENTS!

T HE SMELL OF FLOWERS WOULD BE STRONGER
AND I COULD SMELL THE SPRINGTIME LONGER."

A ND SO I PUT THE SECOND NOSE IN PLACE
RIGHT NEXT TO THE ONE ALREADY ON MY FACE.

Then I inhaled a whale inhale
and filled my nostrils like four sails
and in them rushed a rush of air
that carried smells from everywhere.

I SMELLED THE APPLES GROWING ON TREES AND HONEY MADE IN HIVES BY HONEY BEES.

I SMELLED BREAD RISING IN BAKERS' OVENS ALONG WITH BATCHES OF BLUEBERRY MUFFINS.

AND FROM THE PARK CAME WAFTING TO MY NOSES
THE DELICATE SCENT OF DEEP RED ROSES
THE KIND THAT GROW IN ROWS
BESIDE ONE'S TOESES.

Down the block I smelled a candy store
packed with chocolates, caramels, lollipops and more.

AND DOWN THE STREET I SMELLED A FEAST
A MEAL TO FEED, OH, TWENTY AT LEAST!
WITH CREAMCHEESE SOUP AND JAM ON RYE
PICKLES AND FRUIT AND MARSHMALLOW PIE
BROCCOLI SPEARS IN ARTICHOKE SAUCE
AND A MUSTARD SANDWICH WITH EXTRA MOSS.

ALL OF THESE SMELLS WERE MAKING ME HUNGRY
WHEN SUDDENLY A NEW BATCH OF SMELLS STUNG ME.
I BREATHED IN DEEPER SO I COULD SEE
JUST WHAT THESE BRAND NEW SMELLS COULD BE.

I SMELLED PAST THE APPLES AND HONEY AND BREAD—
PAST THE PARK WITH ROSES ALL RED
PAST THE STORE FILLED WITH CANDY, AND ON PAST THE FEAST
AND I KEPT ON SMELLING DUE NORTH BY NORTHEAST.

I SMELLED OVER HIGHWAYS AND BYWAYS OF CARS
OVER RIVERS AND FORESTS AND SKIES FULL OF STARS.

OVER BIG HILLS AND SMALL HILLS AND VALLEYS AND PEAKS
I SMELLED FOR WHAT SEEMED TO BE WEEKS UPON WEEKS.

I SMELLED THE IGUANAS THAT PLAYED IN THE TREES.
I SMELLED DUST AND POLLEN THAT DANCED ON THE BREEZE.

I SMELLED SOMEONE READING A VERY LONG BOOK
WHILE DANGLING HER FEET IN AN ICY COLD BROOK.

I SMELLED A MAN GROWING A BEARD TWELVE-FEET LONG
AND ANOTHER MAN SINGING A TWELVE-FOOT-LONG SONG.

I SMELLED PANDAS CHEWING BAMBOO STICKS IN CHINA.
I SMELLED A TRAIN WHISTLE IN NORTH CAROLINA.

I SMELLED ON FOR MILES AND MILES AND MILES
THROUGH JUNGLES AND SWAMPS FILLED WITH FIERCE CROCODILES.

THROUGH BEACHES OF SAND AND OCEANS OF SHARKS
I KEPT ON SMELLING THROUGH LIGHT AND THROUGH DARK.

I SMELLED A GREAT OAK TREE WITH OWLS LIVING IN IT AND SO MANY OTHER NEW SMELLS EVERY MINUTE.

AND JUST WHEN I THOUGHT THAT I'D SMELLED EVERY SMELL
EVERY PLACE, EVERY THING, EVERY ANT AND GAZELLE
I DETECTED A FINAL SCENT QUITE UNFAMILIAR
LIKE NOTHING THAT I'D EVER SMELLED, BUT MUCH CHILLIER.

DETERMINED TO FIND THE ODD SMELL'S SOURCE
I FOCUSED MY NOSES WITH ALL OF THEIR FORCE.

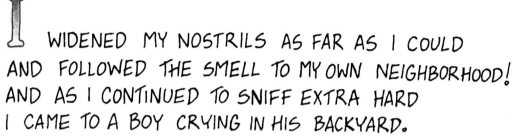

I WIDENED MY NOSTRILS AS FAR AS I COULD
AND FOLLOWED THE SMELL TO MY OWN NEIGHBORHOOD!
AND AS I CONTINUED TO SNIFF EXTRA HARD
I CAME TO A BOY CRYING IN HIS BACKYARD.

"WHY ARE YOU CRYING?" I ASKED THE YOUNG BOY. "THERE'S SO MUCH TO SMELL, YOU SHOULD BE JUMPING FOR JOY!"

"BUT DAT'S JUST DEH THIGG," HE SAID WITH A TEAR.
"I HAVE LOST MBY NDOSE, AND I'MB NDOT QUITE SURE WHERE."
THEN HE LOOKED AT MY NOSES WITH A GREAT DEAL OF CARE.
"BUT YOU CAD HELP MBE. SINCE YOU'VE GOT A SPARE ONDE
PERHAPS YOU COULD FIND IT IND YOUR HEART TO SHARE ONDE!"

AND JUST THEN I REALIZED THAT THE STRANGE SMELL HAD BEEN
THE SMELL OF THIS BOY WITH NO NOSE AND NO GRIN.

ALL AT ONCE MY BODY TURNED ORANGE WITH GREED
AND I THOUGHT TO MYSELF, "BOTH THESE NOSES I NEED.
HOW ELSE CAN MY SENSES TRULY BE FREED?
AFTER ALL, IT'S NOT AS THOUGH I EXCEED
THE NUMBER OF NOSES A PERSON SHOULD HOLD."
AND I LOOKED AT MY NOSES, BOTH THE NEW AND THE OLD.

So LOVELY THEY SAT IN THEIR NOSE-SITTING PLACE
SUCH STYLE! SUCH POISE! SUCH ELEGANT GRACE!
THEN I LOOKED AT THE BOY WITH NO NOSE ON HIS FACE
AND I SAID TO MYSELF, "WHAT A DISGRACE!
TO GIVE HIM A NOSE WOULD JUST BE A WASTE.
FOR ANY BOY WHO COULD LOSE THE NOSE ON HIS FACE
CANNOT HAVE TRUE NOSE-HAVING TASTE."

BUT JUST AS I THOUGHT THIS THOUGHT FILLED WITH GREED
THERE CAME A SUDDEN GUSTY BREEZE
THAT MADE ME CLOSE MY EYES AND SNEEZE *THE BIGGEST SNEEZE...*

AAAACHHOOOOOOOOOOO!!!!!!

ND I OPENED MY EYES JUST IN TIME TO SEE
TWO DARK TINY OBJECTS FLY AWAY FROM ME.

"OH NDO!" I SAID AS I RACED UP TO TRACE
MY FINGERS ALONG MY NOSE—SITTING PLACE.
BUT I WAS TOO LATE.
I HAD SNEEZED BOTH NOSES CLEAR OFF OF MY FACE.

AND I LOOKED AT THE BOY OF WHOM I'D MADE FUN
AND HIS ONCE NOSELESS FACE NOW SHONE IN THE SUN
AS I SAW MY TWO NOSES ON HIS FACE OF ONE!

"GOODNDESS MBE! WHAT HAVE I DONDE!
I ONCE HAD TWO NDOSES AND NDOW I HAVE NDONDE!"

With that the boy turned to me quite surprised.
"Thank you," he said. "Two noses are plenty."
And as he left, this lesson I realized

"Better happy with one nose than to be without any."

3/97